Five reasons why you'll love Isadora Moon ...

Meet the magical,
fang-tastic Isadora Moon!

Isadora's cuddly toy, Pink Rabbit,
has been magicked to life!

Get ready for some
magical mischief!

Isadora's family is crazy!

Enchanting
pink and black
pictures

What makes you feel better when you're feeling poorly?

Tucked up in bed watching my favourite TV shows!
Tommy, age 7

Ice cream, hot milk, and hugging my favourite teddy!
Laura, age 8

Squishing up with all my fluffy teddies!
Emilia, age 9

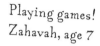

Dress costumes
and playing with
my big sis.
Diana, age 7

Playing games!
Zahavah, age 7

Eating fruit,
especially kiwi fruit!
Luna, age 7

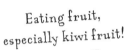

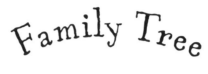

Family Tree

My Mum
Countess Cordelia
Moon

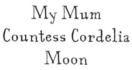

Baby Honeyblossom

My Dad
Count Bartholomew
Moon

Me!
Isadora Moon

Pink Rabbit

For vampires, fairies and humans everywhere!

OXFORD
UNIVERSITY PRESS

Great Clarendon Street, Oxford OX2 6DP
Oxford University Press is a department of the University of Oxford.
It furthers the University's objective of excellence in research, scholarship,
and education by publishing worldwide. Oxford is a registered trade mark
of Oxford University Press in the UK and in certain other countries

Text copyright © Harriet Muncaster 2022
Illustrated by Harriet Muncaster and Rob Parkinson

The moral rights of the author have been asserted

Database right Oxford University Press (maker)

First published in 2022

British Library Cataloguing in Publication Data

Data available

ISBN:978-0-19277356-2

5 7 9 10 8 6 4

Printed in Great Britain by Bell and Bain Ltd, Glasgow

The manufacturing process conforms to the environmental
regulations of the country of origin.

MIX
Paper from
responsible sources
FSC® C007785
www.fsc.org

ISADORA MOON

Gets the Magic Pox

Harriet Muncaster

OXFORD
UNIVERSITY PRESS

Chapter ONE

It was Friday afternoon and I was happily sitting at my desk with Pink Rabbit snoozing on my lap when Miss Cherry announced some worrying news.

'On Monday morning,' she said, 'we are going to have a maths test!'

I felt my insides squiggle with nerves.

A test! I hated tests.

'I want you to spend the weekend brushing up on your times tables,' said Miss Cherry.

I glanced at my best friend Zoe who was sitting at the desk next to me, but she didn't look worried at all. But then

Zoe is good at everything. Maths is my least favourite subject and times tables are really hard to remember.

I felt completely disheartened as I packed my books into my satchel to go home.

'What's the matter?' asked Zoe as we walked out into the playground.

'I'm just a bit worried about the test,' I admitted. 'Vampire fairies aren't very good at maths.'

'You'll be fine Isadora!' said Zoe, sneezing into a tissue. 'Times tables are easy anyway.'

'They are for *you!*' I said.

'You're really good at them!'

'That's just because I practice them a lot,' said Zoe. 'My mum bought me a special CD with times tables songs on it. We listen to it every morning in the car. Maths can be really fun if you give it a chance. Putting numbers together is kind of like doing a puzzle!'

I frowned.

'I'll lend you my CD if you like,' said Zoe kindly. 'I already know it off by heart.'

'Oh no, that's OK,' I said quickly. The idea of listening to songs about times tables would just make me feel more anxious. I didn't fancy that at all!

Zoe shrugged.

'You can phone me over the weekend if you change your mind,' she said. 'Oh look, there's my mum! Bye Isadora!' and then she ran off across the playground.

I walked slowly over to where my mum was standing with my baby sister Honeyblossom in her pushchair. My mum is a fairy and I knew she wouldn't really understand about maths tests. They learn very different sorts of subjects at fairy school: wand waving, toadstool foraging, and ballet mostly.

'Hello, darling!' smiled Mum as I hurried over to her. 'How was your day?'

'Fine,' I said, deciding that there was no point in telling her about the maths test. 'It was Bruno's birthday. He brought in a cake!'

'How lovely!' said Mum as we began to walk towards the school gates and out onto the pavement.

'It was strawberry flavoured,' I said.

I continued to tell Mum all the other

things about my day as we walked along but still, at the back of my mind, I couldn't help thinking of the maths test. There was no way of getting out of doing it unless I was ill on Monday.

Mum started telling me all the funny things that Honeyblossom had done that day, but I was only half listening. My mind was whirring. Did I *really* dare to pretend I was ill on Monday?

No . . . I could never!

. . . or could I?

As soon as I got home I went straight to the kitchen for my favourite snack—a slice of toast and peanut butter. Dad was already up from his daily sleep—he's a vampire so he sleeps a lot during the day. He was sitting at the table drinking his favourite red juice.

'Good day at school, Isadora?' he asked.

'Yes, thanks Dad,' I said as I dropped
a slice of bread into the toaster. 'I was
wondering if I could call Mirabelle tonight?'

'Mirabelle?' said Mum looking a little

wary. Mirabelle is my cousin. She's half fairy and half witch and very mischievous. She often gets me into trouble even when she doesn't mean to, but I still love spending time with her. She's so much fun!

'I haven't spoken to her for a while,' I said. 'Can I? Please? It is Friday!'

'Well, I suppose so,' said Mum.

'I don't see why not,' said Dad.

Once I had eaten my snack I ran into the hallway where the crystal ball is kept on a little table by the front door. Mum waved her wand over it, muttering my cousin Mirabelle's number and it began to glow with a rosy pink light. Fog swirled inside the crystal and I stared eagerly

into its depths, knowing that it would be making a ringing sound in Mirabelle's house right that moment! I hoped that she was in. After a few minutes, the fog cleared and suddenly I could see my Uncle Alvin's face peering at us from inside the sphere.

'Ah!' he said. 'Cordelia! My dear sister. How are you?'

Mum and Uncle Alvin began to chat, and I hopped up and down impatiently waiting for them to finish. Eventually Mum said, 'Isadora was hoping to speak to Mirabelle.'

'That young rascal!' said Uncle Alvin. 'She's just put a slug in poor Wilbur's shoe. I'll go and fetch her.' Then he disappeared for a moment. Mum wandered off back to the kitchen and I found myself alone in the hallway. I hugged Pink Rabbit tightly and gleefully and he squirmed in my arms.

'Isadora!' said Mirabelle as she suddenly appeared inside the crystal ball. 'How are you?'

'I'm fine thanks,' I grinned. 'I wanted to ask you a favour!'

'A favour?' said Mirabelle, and I saw her eyes glint with mischief.

'Yes,' I whispered. 'I might need to be ill on Monday. There's a maths test I want to avoid. I thought you'd probably know some kind of witchy potion I could maybe use to make me look ill so Mum and Dad let me stay at home!'

'Hmm,' said Mirabelle, and her eyebrows knotted together wickedly. 'I do know some skiving spells.'

Skiving spells. I wasn't sure I liked that word.

'I don't want to

skive school,' I said hurriedly. 'I'm not doing it to be naughty. I just want to miss the test!'

'It's still skiving Isadora,' whispered Mirabelle. 'You can't pretend it's not!'

'I suppose,' I said, shuffling my feet uncomfortably. 'Well, I might not use the potion. I just wanted to have it, in case.'

'I must say, I am surprised at you,' said Mirabelle.

'Yes, well . . .' I said, thinking about how panicky I felt the last time we did a maths test. 'I'm not saying I would definitely do it, I just think it's good to have options!'

Mirabelle shrugged.

'OK,' she said.

'Well listen. I know three spells you could use. One of them will give you the magic pox—you'll get pink spots all over your skin. They last a couple of days. There's another spell I know that will make you cough up frogs for a week. I wouldn't recommend that one, to be honest. And then the last one will give you a bad case of witch lice— tiny little beetles in pointed hats that set up home in your hair. Very itchy!'

'Ugh! I don't like the sound of any of those spells but I suppose the magic pox would be the best of the three,' I said doubtfully.

'Yes,' agreed Mirabelle. 'I'd go with the magic pox. And at least it will make you look ill even if you don't feel it! Have you got a pen and paper? I can tell you the ingredients for the spell. You need to do it at night time, out in the garden, under the light of the moon.'

'OK,' I said, grabbing a pen from next to the crystal ball and beginning to scribble down the ingredients onto a pad of paper. As I did so I felt an uncomfortable prickling sensation run up and down my spine. I wasn't used to breaking the rules. But it was a last resort!

Ingredients

5 strawberries

1 squirt of Shaving cream

1 handful of red rose petals

A bar of pink soap
shaved down into flakes

A sprinkle of stardust

'You probably have all those ingredients lying around somewhere,' said Mirabelle. 'There are hardly any specialist witchy ones in it and your dad loves astronomy. He's bound to have some stardust! It's an easy spell to make. Go outside at midnight and mix everything up under the light of the moon. Then rub the potion onto your face and go to sleep. You'll wake up with the magic pox! Do it tomorrow night and the spots will be there all Sunday and Monday but they'll be gone by Tuesday, so you can go back to school.'

'OK!' I said, starting to feel a little bit excited despite myself. 'Don't tell your mum and dad will you Mirabelle?'

'Of course I won't!' scoffed Mirabelle.
'I . . . ARGH!!!' suddenly she screamed as
my cousin Wilbur appeared right behind
her and dropped a large spider right down
the neck of her dress. Mirabelle hopped
about screeching.

'I'll get you Wilbur!' she shouted,
disappearing from view.
'Just you wait!'

I stared into the depths of the crystal ball as the pink fog began to swirl again and then fade to nothing. I folded up my ingredients list carefully and popped it into my pocket. I would spend the following day finding the ingredients and getting everything ready for the spell just in *case* I decided to use it.

Chapter TWO

After breakfast the next day I began
my mission. The easiest thing to find
would be the red rose petals. Fairies love
nature so Mum makes sure our garden
is always blooming. I found a rose bush
and plucked a few petals off each of the
roses, dropping them into a basket. Mum
would never notice! Then I hurried

upstairs to the bathroom
where Dad keeps all his
shaving things. I found an
unopened can of shaving
foam in the cupboard and a
bar of pink soap
so I put them

both in my basket too. Next, I
ran all the way up the twirly
steps of the second tallest
turret of our house where
Dad's astronomy tower is

to find the stardust. There
was a jar of it on a shelf so
I took a small pinch. The
last thing to find was the

32

strawberries. Mum always has loads of fruit and vegetables in the house so I knew there would be some in the fridge. I took five and popped them into my basket when no one was looking. Then I scurried up to my bedroom and hid the basket of potion ingredients under my bed.

That evening, after I had kissed Mum and Dad goodnight, I lay in bed with my eyes wide open feeling nervous and guilty. I really didn't want to do the maths test on Monday but I didn't know if I could actually go through with the spell.

I kept looking at the clock on my

bedside table, watching it tick towards midnight.

I heard Dad leave the house for his nightly vampire fly and I heard Mum go into her bedroom and shut the door. Everything was quiet and still in my room and a sliver of moonlight shone through the gap in my curtains, leaving a glowing line along my floor.

Perhaps I would just take the potion into the garden and see how I felt then? At twenty minutes to midnight, I slipped out of bed, leaving Pink Rabbit snoozing, curled up in a ball. I put on my dressing gown, grabbed the basket of potion ingredients, and tiptoed down the stairs to the kitchen. The house felt strange with all the lights off and I gave a little shiver as I opened the kitchen cabinet to find one of Mum's mixing bowls and a wooden spoon. All was quiet as I unlocked the back door and hurried out into the back

garden. The only
sound I could hear
was the hooting of an owl nearby. It didn't
scare me. I am half vampire.

'I'll just *make* the potion to see if
I want to use it,' I thought as I knelt
down on the grass and put the mixing
bowl in front of me, making sure that the
moonlight was shining into it. I began to
fill it with the potion ingredients, starting
with the soap flakes and finishing up
with a big fluffy squirt of shaving foam.
I maybe squirted a little *too* much of the
shaving foam into the bowl but it was so
much fun, pressing the top of the can!

I mixed everything together enjoying
how the mixture began to fizz and bubble
and twinkle. It smelt lovely! When it was
finished I stared into the bowl, breathing

in the sweet rosy scent. Did I dare to put it on my face? *Should I?*

As I stared at the mixture the fluffy, foamy bubbles began to deflate a little. I needed to use it quickly. It was now or never! Without letting myself think too much more about it, I scooped some of the

potion out with my hands and rubbed it into my cheeks, pretending that I was my glamourous witch aunt, Seraphina, putting on her face cream. It felt cool and soothing against my skin. Then I tipped the rest of the mixture out, making sure it was well hidden under a bush, washed up Mum's mixing bowl and spoon, and scurried up the stairs back to bed. I lay under the covers, shivering from the cold night air but also from fear and excitement. I had done it! I had done it! No maths test for me on Monday!

'Isadooora!' came Mum's voice through my dreams the next morning. 'What has happened to your face!'

I sat up in bed, rubbing my eyes. The sun was already streaming through my window. I must have woken up late.

I stared at Mum, confused for a moment, and then remembered creeping out to the garden to make my potion in the middle of the night.

The magic pox! That's what must have happened to my face. I started to get out of bed, but Mum gently pushed me back down.

'Oh no!' she said. 'You're not well Isadora. You need to stay in bed! You've got a bad case of . . . *something*. I'm going to go and fetch Dad!'

As soon as Mum had left the room I jumped out of bed and ran over to my mirror, gasping as I caught sight of my face. It was covered in bright pink spots. I definitely had

41

the magic pox.

'*Oh!*' I said out loud. It felt rather shocking to see myself looking so ill. But I didn't feel ill. I felt fine! Except for a very slight headache and stuffy nose.

I leapt back into bed as I heard Mum and Dad coming back up the stairs.

'Oh dear, oh dear!' said Dad when he saw my face. 'You've got . . .' he scratched his head. 'What's that illness that human children get? The duckling pox! You must have caught it at school Isadora.'

'*Chicken pox!*' corrected Mum. 'But it doesn't look like chicken pox to me. It's too . . . pink! Maybe it's a magical illness. We did go to that fairy wedding last weekend, maybe Isadora caught it there!'

'Well, whatever it is she needs lots of rest today,' said Dad. 'And tomorrow too I should think.'

'OK,' I said, trying to stop myself

from smiling. I had done it! I was going to get to stay off school on Monday.

I slid out of bed and hurried over to my wardrobe to get dressed.

'What are you doing?' said Mum. 'You need to stay in your pyjamas and go and sit on the sofa!'

'But we always go to the park on Sunday morning!' I said. 'I think I can just about manage to go to the park.'

'Oh no!' said Dad, shaking his head. 'Absolutely not. You mustn't overexert yourself when you're ill. Down to the sofa you go!'

I followed Mum and Dad downstairs, suddenly feeling a bit despondent. It was so

sunny outside. It was such a lovely day for
going to the park!

I sat down on the sofa and wrapped
myself in my duvet, gazing outside
longingly at the sunshine. Mum plonked
Honeyblossom down on the floor and she
started to play with her blocks.

'I'll just go and make you some

breakfast,' said Mum, disappearing out of the room. 'Something full of nutrients! Oh, you poor little thing!'

Ten minutes later Mum and Dad came back into the room carrying a tray. On it was a bowl of Mum's special healthy muesli with lots of nuts and seeds in it and a glass of Dad's special red vampire juice.

'*Red juice!*' I said, staring in horror at the glass. 'You know I hate red juice!'

'But it's the healthiest thing for a sick vampire to drink,' said Dad. 'And you are half vampire!'

'But . . .' I began.

'No buts!' said Dad. 'Make sure you drink it all up!'

Once Mum and Dad had disappeared back to the kitchen again, I jumped off the sofa and hurried over to the window. Opening it a crack, I tipped the glass of red juice out onto the flowerbed below. It made me feel very naughty, but there was no way I could drink it! A worrying thought suddenly occurred to me. *Was I turning into Mirabelle?* I hoped not! As I emptied the glass, I noticed something strange

in the garden. The bush under which I had tipped all the leftover potion was covered all over with bright pink buds. They looked kind of . . . fluffy! And they definitely hadn't been there yesterday. It looked as though the bush had the magic pox too!

Oh dear, I thought. *I hope Mum and*

Dad don't notice!

Suddenly, I didn't feel like my plan was going very well at all. I wasn't allowed to go to the park and I had to eat a horrid breakfast and now I also had to stop Mum and Dad from looking out into the back garden too! Hurriedly, I drew the curtains. The room was now dim and dark. Honeyblossom's little face crumpled up and she started to cry.

'What's going on?' asked Mum, whisking back into the room. 'Why have you closed the curtains, Isadora? Have you got a headache?'

'Yes,' I said. It wasn't a lie. I was starting to get a headache. But it wasn't from the magic pox. It was from all this stress!

'I'll take Honeyblossom to the park,' said Mum, 'and leave you in peace, Isadora. Dad's going to bed for his daily sleep, but you can wake him if you need anything.'

'OK,' I nodded, wishing that I could go to the park too.

I listened wistfully to the sound

of Mum getting Honeyblossom into her little hat and wellies. Then the front door closed and there was silence in the house.

I wished I had something interesting to do. I wished I had a TV like Zoe has in her house! I lay on the sofa under my duvet feeling very, very bored. I almost started to regret doing the spell at all! The idea of doing a maths test wasn't sounding quite so horrible now that I was stuck indoors with the curtains closed on such a lovely, sunny day. After a while I threw off my duvet and went back over to the window, twitching the curtains back. The bush was still covered in pink spots and they looked bigger and fluffier than before! I started to feel a little worried. Maybe I should go outside and have a look? Mum and Honeyblossom were out and Dad was asleep. No one needed to know I had got off the sofa. I slipped on my shoes and made my way out into the back garden. Now I was a bit closer I could see that the pink fluffy balls had eyes! Big blinky eyes that were staring at me.

'*Oh no!*' I whispered.

I hadn't disposed of the spell properly. It probably wasn't supposed to be put on the roots of a bush. I peered closely at one of the fluffy balls. It was quite cute really.

It had two pink pointy ears, a little button nose and . . . it was bouncing right off the bush towards me! I stepped back, catching it in my hands and feeling its soft fur. Then it bounced off my hands and onto the grass, making its way towards the back door of the house.

'Wait!' I cried, but

the fluffy ball didn't stop and bounced through the back door, disappearing into the house. And now all the other fluffballs were following it too. They were jumping off the bush and swarming towards the back door. And then I started to notice something else. Everything that the fluffy balls touched began to get pink spots. The grass had pink spots. The doormat had pink spots. The garden path had pink spots!

'Oh no!' I squeaked again, and ran back into the house, closing the door behind me to stop any more of them following me in. But it was too late. There were already loads of them in the house. They were pinging off the walls and bouncing down the hallway. Everything was covered in pink spots.

I didn't know how to get rid of the little creatures but I needed to do something about them fast before Mum and Honeyblossom got back from the park. Where was my wand? Maybe I could wave it and see if they disappeared? I had no idea if it would work but decided I had to try.

I began to run up the stairs just as I heard a sound that made my blood run cold. A key in the lock. Mum and Honeyblossom were back!

I stared around me at the spotty house and at all the little fluffballs bouncing around. And then I turned around and RAN. I ran all the way up the stairs and into my bedroom where I slammed the door shut and slid under the bed. My heart was racing and I felt shaky all over.

What had I done?

Chapter
THREE

I lay under the bed for what felt like an
age.

I felt terrible.

'Isadooooora!' I heard Mum yelling
from downstairs. 'Isadooora! Where are
you?'

I closed my eyes tight, hoping
that everything would just go away but

eventually I heard the sound of Mum's footsteps coming up the stairs and her feet appeared standing right by my bed.

'Isadora Moon,' she said in the sort of voice that didn't sound like she was happy at all. 'Come out from under the bed.'

61

I slid out with my eyes still tightly
closed.

'What in the name of sugarplums is
going on?' said Mum.

I opened my eyes and noticed that my
bedroom was now covered in spots and
three of the fluffballs were bouncing on

the bed. Mum put Honeyblossom down on the floor and my baby sister immediately toddled towards the bed, reaching out her chubby hands to grab one of the fluffballs.

'Don't touch it Honeyblossom!' I warned, but it was too late. Suddenly Honeyblossom sprung out in pink spots. Mum stared at her and narrowed her eyes.

'I know what this is!' she said. 'Isadora Moon you are not ill at all! You've been using magic!'

I stared back at Mum feeling both dismayed and relieved

all at once.

'It's the magic pox,' I admitted. 'I'm really sorry.'

Mum stared around at all the fluff balls now bouncing into my bedroom and sighed. She looked really disappointed.

I felt awful.

Honeyblossom had grabbed onto another fluffball now and was clutching it to her chest,

burying her face into its soft fur and cooing.

'I don't know how to get rid of them,' I said in a small voice. 'I didn't mean to make them appear! I just wanted to give myself the magic pox, that's all!'

Mum pursed her lips, glancing up at the curtains where two of the fluffballs were having a grand time swinging back and forth.

'They're pretty harmless creatures,' said Mum. 'They're just a side effect of the spell. They will disappear when the spots disappear I should think. At least Honeyblossom is enjoying them. It's not the fluffballs I'm worried about though

Isadora. It's the fact that you lied to me and Dad! That's not like you at all!'

'I know,' I said in a small voice. 'I really am sorry.'

'Why?' asked Mum.

'I have a maths test at school tomorrow,' I said. 'I'm not very good at maths. I wanted to be ill so I could stay at home.'

Mum frowned.

'Why do you think you're not good at maths?' she asked.

'Because I'm a vampire fairy,' I said. 'I'm just not naturally very good at it. They don't learn maths at vampire and fairy school. It's not in my genes!'

Mum
threw her head
back and laughed.

'Of course they teach maths
at vampire and fairy school!' she
said. 'How else would fairies know how
many toadstools to put in a fairy ring?
How else would vampires be able to
navigate the hundreds of stars in the sky
at night? How else would I know how
much flour and sugar to put in my cakes?'

I stared at Mum feeling a bit foolish.

'And besides,' continued Mum. 'Even
if you're not naturally good at something
you can get good at it by practising. Being
good at something isn't just about talent.

It's also about working hard at it! I never see you practising your times tables! I'd be happy to help you if you asked!'

'Oh!' I said. The thought had never occurred to me before. Maybe I could get better at my times tables if I practised them. Maybe it didn't matter about my vampire-fairy genes!

'Why don't we practise your times tables together today?' said Mum. 'And then even if you don't do well in the test tomorrow, at least you know you'll have done your best. You can't do better than your best! And I can assure you that if you practise you will do better in the test than if you hadn't practised at all.'

'OK,' I nodded, feeling optimistic. 'And maybe I could get a CD too! Zoe has a CD with times tables songs on it.'

'Hmm . . .' said Mum. 'I might be able to do better than a CD . . .'

I followed Mum downstairs into the spotty kitchen and we sat down at the spotty kitchen table. All around us the fluff balls bounced about and Honeyblossom tried to catch them with her chubby little hands. Mum got out her wand and pointed it at the radio. The sound of bouncy music filled the air. Then Mum pointed her wand towards the fruit bowl. Two oranges began to dance upwards towards the ceiling. Mum zapped

them with her wand in a flurry of sparks
so that they multiplied.

'Two oranges, times two oranges . . .'
she sang.

'Is FOUR oranges!' I yelled.

'Well done!' said Mum, beginning to dance around the kitchen. I followed her and together we sang and danced our way through the times tables. It was much more fun than I could ever have imagined. Eventually, I found I could remember some of the times tables without even looking at all the fruit dancing in the air. I was starting to see how they worked inside my head.

'It is a bit like a puzzle!' I said, remembering what Zoe had told me.

'Yes!' said Mum. 'Maths can be a bit like doing a puzzle. That's a good way of thinking about it, Isadora.'

After practising for an hour, I found
I could answer lots of the times tables
questions that Mum asked me correctly
and I was feeling really proud of myself.
I realized I was actually looking forward
to the test on Monday! It was a strange
feeling. But I wanted to show off what I
had learned.

'You can't go to school with all
those spots on your face though, Isadora,'
said Mum. 'We had better try and reverse
the magic you used if you want to do the
maths test. It doesn't look like it's going to
wear off by tomorrow.'

'No,' I agreed. 'Mirabelle did say the
spell would last for a couple of days.'

'*Mirabelle!*' said Mum, rolling her eyes. 'I should have known! It's a witch spell. We had better ring Aunt Seraphina on the crystal ball. Maybe there's a way to get rid of all the fluffballs too.'

At the mention of the fluffballs disappearing, Honeyblossom burst into tears.

'Oh dear,' soothed Mum. 'I think she's become rather attached but they are becoming a bit of a nuisance. One just knocked over my cup of tea!'

I followed Mum

74

out to the hallway and watched as she waved her wand over the crystal ball again, muttering my aunt and uncle's number. Soon the pink fog cleared and Aunt Seraphina's face popped up.

'Cordelia!' she said. 'How nice to see you!'

'And you!' said Mum. 'I've just got a quick question. Is there a way to reverse the magic pox spell before it naturally comes to an end? We have a bit of a . . . situation over here.'

'The magic pox!' said Aunt Seraphina. 'Bouncing bats! I haven't used that spell in years! Not since I used to skive off . . . oh, er, I mean . . . yes there might be something you can do. How in the name of frogspawn did you know how to do that kind of witch spell?'

'Oh, er . . .' said Mirabelle, sidling into view. 'I told Isadora how to do it.'

Aunt Seraphina shook her head in exasperation.

'Let me get my spell book,' she said.

Mirabelle grinned into the crystal ball.

'Isadora!' she hooted. 'Just look at your spotty face!'

I grinned back.

'I have the magic pox!' I said. 'But I want to undo the spell now. I've changed my mind. I'm going to do the maths test tomorrow!'

Mirabelle nodded, then she peered in closer to her crystal ball.

'What are those fluffy things bouncing around your house?' she asked.

'I'm not sure,' I said. 'They grew on the branches of a bush in our garden. I poured the leftover spell mixture underneath it.'

'Oh!' said Mirabelle and her face went

a little pink. 'Sorry! I forgot to tell you to dispose of the mixture properly. Down the sink would have been best. It must have slipped my mind!'

I saw Mum roll her eyes again just as Aunt Seraphina came back into view. She opened a large spell book and tapped at a page with her long black witch nails.

'Here,' she said.

Mum peered at the page and scribbled down everything it said to do. Then she and Seraphina had a long chat which was boring so I took the piece of paper that Mum had written all the ingredients down on and began to look for all the things we needed.

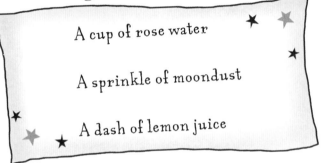

A cup of rose water

A sprinkle of moondust

A dash of lemon juice

By the time Mum had finished on the crystal ball, I had everything ready. Mum and I mixed all the ingredients up in a bowl. It was a very sloshy, watery sort of potion. Mum poured it into two empty spray bottles.

'Close your eyes Isadora!' she said. I closed my eyes and felt a cooling spritz of potion land on my face. When I opened them again and looked in the mirror, the spots had gone!

'That was easy,' laughed Mum. 'Now we just have to do Honeyblossom, all the fluffballs, and if there's any potion left, the whole house!'

Together, we began to chase the fluffballs.

SPRITZ!

'Got one!' I shouted triumphantly, as a fluffball disappeared in a pink puff of smoke.

'Me too!' shouted Mum as she lunged towards another fluffball that was bouncing across the hallway.

I was glad Honeyblossom had now gone down for her nap. I think she would have been quite upset to see her beloved fluffballs disappearing like this!

'What is going on?' asked Dad when he came downstairs from his daily sleep. 'Why is everything looking so . . . spotty?

And Isadora you look remarkably well compared to this morning! That red juice must have done wonders for your health! I shall start making you drink it more often.'

'It's a long story,' said Mum as she pointed her bottle of potion at a vase of flowers and spritzed it with a glittering mist. The spots on the roses all disappeared. 'But I think we've just about run out of potion now! At least we've done all the fluffballs so no more spots will appear. We can leave the rest to fade on their own.'

Dad shook his head, confused.

'I don't think I even want to know' he

said, shuffling into the kitchen in his furry
bat slippers. 'I go to sleep for one day . . .'

That night I lay in bed with Pink Rabbit
and hugged him tight. I felt quite excited
about the test tomorrow. It felt good to
have worked hard on something and I
couldn't wait to show Miss Cherry
what I had learned.

Chapter FOUR

The following morning, I woke early.
There was a strange, scratchy feeling at
the back of my throat. I opened my eyes
but the morning sunshine streaming
through the window looked brighter than
usual and it hurt my eyes.

'Morning Isadora!' sang Mum,
skipping into my bedroom in her fairy-like

way. 'Rise and shine!'

I sat up in bed but everything ached
and my nose felt completely stuffy.

'Atishoo!' I said.

Mum glanced at me
and frowned.

'Are you alright Isadora?' she said. 'You seem a little . . . ill.'

'I'm fine!' I said, jumping out of bed. 'Absolutely fine!'

I hurried to my wardrobe and pulled out my school uniform.

'Atishoo!' I said again as I pulled it on.

'Are you sure you're OK?' asked Mum. 'You look pale. Even for you!'

'I'm fine!' I insisted. 'I don't want to miss the maths test. I've practised so hard for it!'

But as I ate my

breakfast I began to feel really dreadful.
My toast tasted like cardboard and I
couldn't even finish eating it.

'I think you're ill!' said Mum. '*Actually*
ill this time! I think you've got a regular
human cold. You must have picked it up at
school last week.'

Now I thought about it, I could remember Zoe sniffing and sneezing a lot on Friday.

'Is there a reversing spell?' I asked hopefully.

'I'm afraid not,' said Mum. 'The only remedy for a bad cold is to have lots of rest and lots of fluid. No school for you today.'

'Oh,' I said sadly, looking down at my plate.

'I'm sorry,' said Mum. 'But there's nothing else for it. Back to the sofa you go!'

I spent the morning wrapped up in my

duvet. Mum brought me drinks of hot lemon and honey and Dad brought me another glass of red juice before he went for his daily sleep. This time I tried to sip it—maybe red juice really would make me feel better! But no, I still couldn't stand the taste.

I felt really disappointed
to be missing the maths test but
sitting snuggled up on the sofa didn't
feel too bad when I was *actually* ill.

'I think Honeyblossom's caught your
cold too,' said Mum, bringing her in and
plonking her down on the sofa. 'She's
all sniffly and grizzly. Oh, my poor little
vampire-fairies.'

'I'll show her some picture books,' I
offered, between sneezes.

Honeyblossom cuddled up to me and
I flicked through a few of her favourite
books, showing her the pictures.
Then I waved my wand and
made some of her favourite

stuffed toys dance around the room. She giggled in delight. It turned out to be quite a nice morning, despite the fact that we were both ill.

By the end of the day both Honeyblossom and I were feeling quite a bit better. Mum looked pleased.

'I think my special fairy honey and lemon drinks have done you both the world of good!' she said. 'I expect you'll be able to go to school tomorrow.'

Chapter FIVE

'Isadora!' said Zoe the following day when I walked into the classroom. 'How was the maths test yesterday?'

I looked at my best friend in confusion.

'I don't know,' I said. 'I wasn't here. I was ill.'

'Oh!' said Zoe. 'I was ill too! I had

a bad sneezy cold. We must have both

missed it.'

Then Miss Cherry came into the room.

'Good morning class!' she beamed. 'I hope everyone's feeling better. We had so many of you off ill yesterday that I decided to postpone the maths test until today!'

I felt a tiny squiggle of nervousness but this time it was mixed in with excitement too.

Miss Cherry handed out paper and pencils.

'Now, there is nothing to worry about,' she said. 'All you have to do is try your best. It's just for me to see how well you're getting on. Nobody will know your score but me.'

Miss Cherry began to read out the questions and I put my head down and focused on the test. Some of the questions were easy and some were hard but I knew that I was getting more right than I would usually. Visions of dancing fruit kept floating into my head, making me smile. It made it easier to think of the right answers! At the end of the test, Miss Cherry said we could mark our own papers. She read out the answers and I only got a few wrong. It felt nice to see quite a few ticks on my piece of paper.

'Woohoo I got full marks!' whooped Zoe from next to me.

'Well done, Zoe,' I smiled.

I hadn't got full marks but I felt really pleased with my result, because I knew I had done my absolute best. Miss Cherry came round to collect our papers.

'Well done Isadora!' she said as she collected mine. 'You did really well today. I know you find maths tricky sometimes.'

I beamed up at my teacher. Miss Cherry knew I had tried my best too.

At the end of the day I ran out happily into the playground towards Mum and Honeyblossom.

'I did really well in my test, Mum!' I said. 'Even Miss Cherry said so!'

'That's great!' said Mum. 'You should be very proud of yourself! Let's go by the ice cream parlour for a celebration on the way home.'

I helped Mum push the pram and we walked all the way into town to the ice cream shop. I chose double chocolate with

raspberry and Mum chose strawberry sorbet. We sat on tall stools and I gobbled mine all up. I noticed that Mum didn't eat much of hers.

'I'm not sure I feel all that well,' she said. *'Atishoo!'*

'Oh dear,' I said. 'You sound a bit . . . ill! You need some nutritious lemon and honey. Come on Mum we'd better get you home!'

When we arrived back at the house, Dad was sitting in the kitchen in his dressing gown and slippers. His usually neatly gelled hair was all messy and ruffled up.

He didn't seem like himself at all!

'I'm feeling a bit off,' he explained. *'Atishoo!'*

I looked at my parents.

'You both need to go and sit on the

sofa under your duvet,' I said. 'I'll bring you all the things you need! And I'll look after Honeyblossom.'

'But you can't make lemon and honey!' sniffled Mum. 'You're too young to use the kettle. 'I'll just magic some up for us.'

'No, no,' I said. 'You mustn't use up your energy Mum. I'll magic it up with my wand and bring it to you very carefully on a tray with some red juice for Dad.'

'OK,' smiled Mum gratefully, and she disappeared upstairs to put on her pyjamas and fetch her duvet. Dad sidled off to the sofa, sneezing.

I unhooked an apron from the peg

behind the door and put it on.

'Come on Pink Rabbit,' I said.
'We have an ill vampire and fairy
to look after!'

Turn the page
for some
Isadorable
things to make
and do!

How to make a fluffball

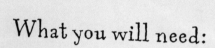

What you will need:

- ⭐ Wool

- ⭐ Cardboard (an old tissue box or cereal packet would work well)

- ⭐ A tin can

- ⭐ A large coin

- ⭐ Sharp scissors

- ⭐ An adult assistant to help with the cutting

- ⭐ Googly eyes

Method:

1. Draw around the tin can, to make a circle on the cardboard.

2. Cut it out.

3. Put the coin in the middle of the circle, and draw around it.

4. Cut a slit from the outer circle to the inner one, and cut out the small circle. You should now have a doughnut shape.

5. Cut a second slit so that you have a gap in your cardboard doughnut. This will make it easier to wrap the wool.

6. Repeat steps 1-5 so that you have two cardboard doughnuts!

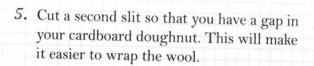

7. Put your cardboard doughnuts together.

8. Start wrapping the wool around and around the doughnut shape until it is completely covered. The thicker you wrap the wool, the fluffier your fluffball will be! Don't cut off the end of your wool yet!

9. Get an adult to slip some sharp scissors between the two cardboard doughnuts, and cut all the way around.

10. Cut off the end of the wool.

11. Cut a length of wool approximately 30cm long.

12. Slip your wool between the two cardboard doughnuts, wrap it around, and tie it very tightly.

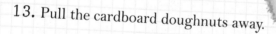

13. Pull the cardboard doughnuts away.

14. Fluff out your fluffball!

15. Trim any long strands of wool.

16. Stick on the googly eyes.

17. Your fluffball is finished!

What to do if you're feeling nervous

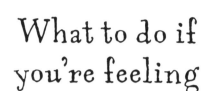

In the story, Isadora is worried
about doing a maths test at school.
Here's how she made herself feel better.

1. She asked for help.

When Isadora told her mum how she was
feeling she started to feel better.

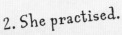

2. She practised.

Being good at something isn't just about talent, it's about working hard at it!

3. She had fun.

Having fun made the worries go away.

4. She tried her best.

It's not the result that matters, it's knowing that you've done your best. You can't do better than that!

Which character are you?

Take the quiz to find out!

You're about to do a test at school. How do you feel?

A. Excited, I love tests!

B. A bit nervous, but I'll try my best.

C. I didn't know there was a test! I'm not ready!

What is your favourite animal?

A. Monkey

B. Rabbit

C. Dragon

How mischievous are you?

A. Not at all, I am always very good.

B. I'm a little bit mischievous, but I try to be good!

C. I am totally mischievous!

Results

Mostly As

You are Zoe! You are always very well behaved, and love to show what you have learned.

Mostly Bs

You are Isadora! You are totally unique, and always try your best!

Mostly Cs

You are Mirabelle! You always have fun, and don't mind getting into a little bit of trouble!

Many more magical stories to collect!

ISADORA MOON

Goes on a School Trip

Half vampire, half fairy, totally unique!

Harriet Muncaster

ISADORA MOON

Goes to the Fair

Half vampire, half fairy, totally unique!

Harriet Muncaster

ISADORA MOON

Gets in Trouble

Half vampire, half fairy, totally unique!

Harriet Muncaster

ISADORA MOON

Makes Winter Magic

Plus fantastic activities!

Half vampire, half fairy, totally unique!

Harriet Muncaster

ISADORA MOON
Has a Sleepover

Half vampire, half fairy, totally unique!
Harriet Muncaster

ISADORA MOON
Puts on a Show

Plus Isadorable activities!

Half vampire, half fairy, totally unique!
Harriet Muncaster

ISADORA MOON
Goes on Holiday

Half vampire, half fairy, totally unique!
Harriet Muncaster

ISADORA MOON
Meets the Tooth Fairy

Half vampire, half fairy, totally unique!
Harriet Muncaster

ISADORA MOON and the Shooting Star

Plus Isadorable activities!

Half vampire, half fairy, totally unique!
Harriet Muncaster

ISADORA MOON Goes to a Wedding

Plus Isadorable activities!

Half vampire, half fairy, totally unique!
Harriet Muncaster

Harriet Muncaster, that's me! I'm the author and illustrator of Isadora Moon. Yes really! I love anything teeny tiny, anything starry, and everything glittery.

ISADORA · MOON

For more activities and
information about the books visit
Isadora Moon on Oxford Owl.
www.isadoramoon.com

For information on the
Isadora Moon animation,
check out the instagram page

@isadoramoon

To visit Harriet Muncaster's website, visit
harrietmuncaster.co.uk

Love Isadora Moon?
Why not try these too . . .

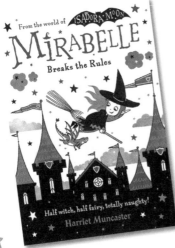